Scaredy Cat

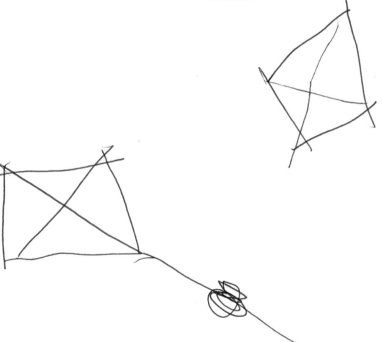

For Judith Grant

ISBN 0-439-09979-X

12 11 10 9 8 7 6 5 4 3   0 1 2 3 4/0

Printed in the U.S.A.   14

First Scholastic printing, March 1999

Scaredy Cat

Joan Rankin

SCHOLASTIC INC.
New York Toronto London Auckland Sydney
Mexico City New Delhi Hong Kong

I don't like
Giants
but …

Mama Meow says
it's only Auntie B.

I am frightened of
Crocodiles
but…

Mama Meow says
they are only Auntie B.'s shoes.

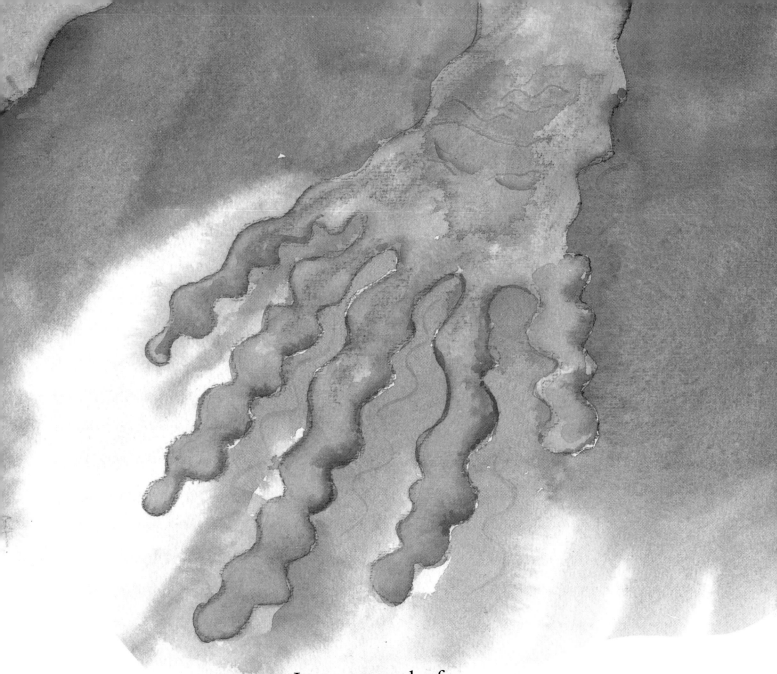

I am scared of

Wiggly Thingamajigs

but…

Mama Meow says
they are only Auntie B.'s hands
wanting to cuddle me.

I am terrified of the

Screaming Sucking Monster

but...

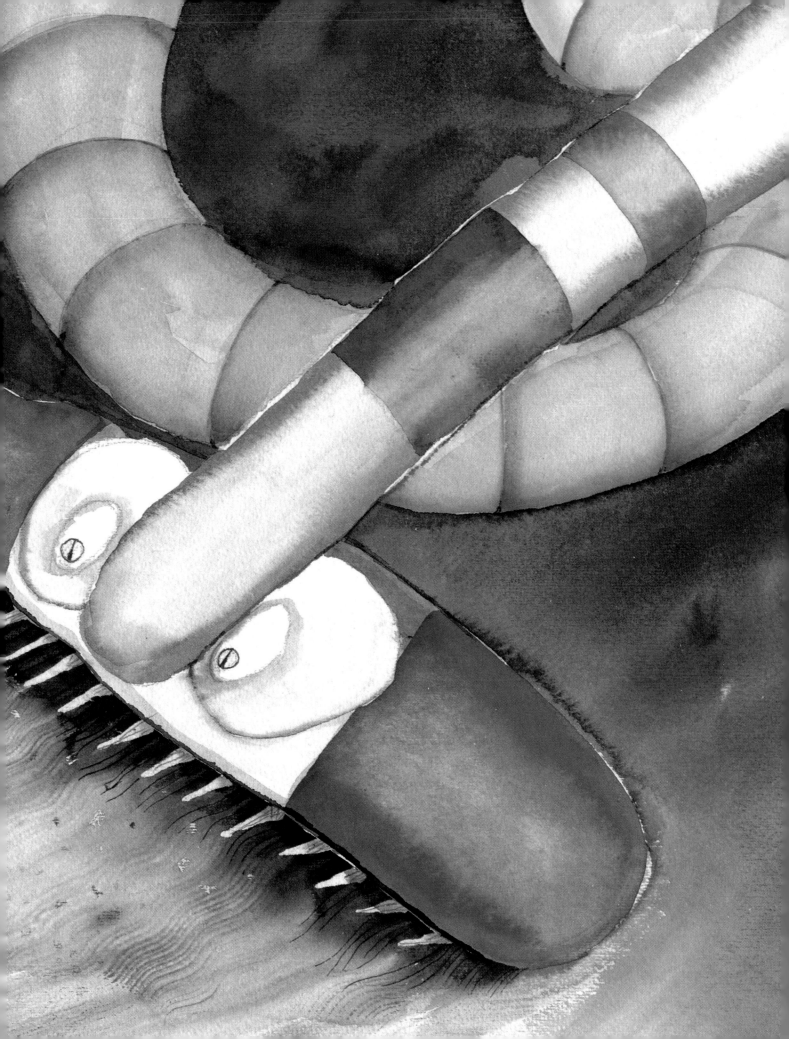

Mama Meow says
it is only Auntie B.'s vacuum cleaner
and Auntie B. won't let it
swallow me.

Ooooh!

A Dark
Hairy Forest!

Quick, quick!
I dash up onto Auntie B.'s lap
and hide in something warm
and woolly.

Auntie B. says
there's no need to worry,
it's only Scratchpooch.
But when *I* look out
all I see is…

an eensie-weensie spider,
looking straight at me.

And if I stretch out my paw…

and fan out my claws…

I can

bonk

that eensie-weensie spider
on his head.

Kapow!

Just listen to him yell!

Mama Meow
says I'm her Tiger Cat
because I'm not scared of

Giants,
Crocodiles,
Wiggly
Thingamajigs,
Screaming Sucking
Monsters,
or A Dark Hairy
Forest.

And

WOW!....

are eensie-weensie spiders
scared of me!